Good Night, Baby Bear

FRANK ASCH

Voyager Books

Harcourt, Inc.

San Diego New York London

Requests for permission to make copies of any part of the work should be mailed to the following address:
Permissions Department, Harcourt, Inc., 6277 Sea Harbor Drive, Orlando, Florida 32887-6777.

www.harcourt.com

First Voyager Books edition 2001
Voyager Books is a trademark of Harcourt, Inc., registered in the United States of America
and/or other jurisdictions.

The Library of Congress has cataloged the hardcover edition as follows:
Asch, Frank.
Good night, Baby Bear/written and illustrated by Frank Asch.
p.   cm.
Summary: As winter approaches, Mother Bear must bring a snack, a drink,
and finally the moon to her cub before he can go to sleep in a cave.
[1. Bears—Fiction. 2. Sleep—Fiction. 3. Bedtime—Fiction. 4. Mother and child—Fiction.] I. Title.
PZ7.A778Gof   1998
[E]—dc21   96-39178
ISBN 0-15-200836-5
ISBN 0-15-216368-9 pb

H G F E D C B

The illustrations in this book were made with brushes
and sponges using Cel-Vinyl acrylic paint on bristol board.
The display type was set in Esprit.
The text type was set in Goudy Catalogue.
Color separations by Tien Wah Press, Singapore
Printed and bound by Tien Wah Press, Singapore
This book was printed on Arctic matte paper.
Production supervision by Sandra Grebenar and Wendi Taylor
Designed by Lydia D'moch

To my mother, Margaret Asch
1916–1997

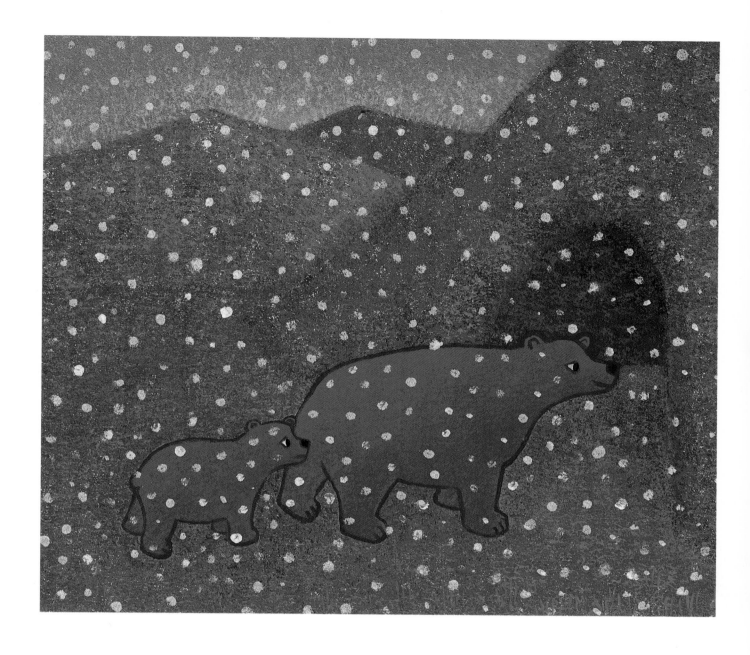

One chilly night as snow began to fall, Mother Bear led
Baby Bear to a cave.

"This is where we'll sleep through the winter," said
Mother Bear.

Baby Bear wasn't used to sleeping in a cave. "Why can't we sleep under the sky like we always do?" he asked.

"Winter has just begun," replied Mother Bear. "Soon it will be too cold to sleep under the sky."

"Mama, I'm hungry," said Baby Bear.

"I'm sorry, there's no food in the cave," replied Mother Bear.

"But I always had a little snack before bedtime when we slept outside," said Baby Bear.

"Mmmm." Mother Bear thought for a moment. "Wait here. I'll be right back."

Not far from the cave, Mother Bear found an old apple tree.

She pulled down a branch, plucked an apple, and carried it back to her cub.

"Thank you, Mama," said Baby Bear as he munched on
the apple.

Mother Bear soon fell asleep. But Baby Bear couldn't
get comfortable. He *couldn't* fall asleep.

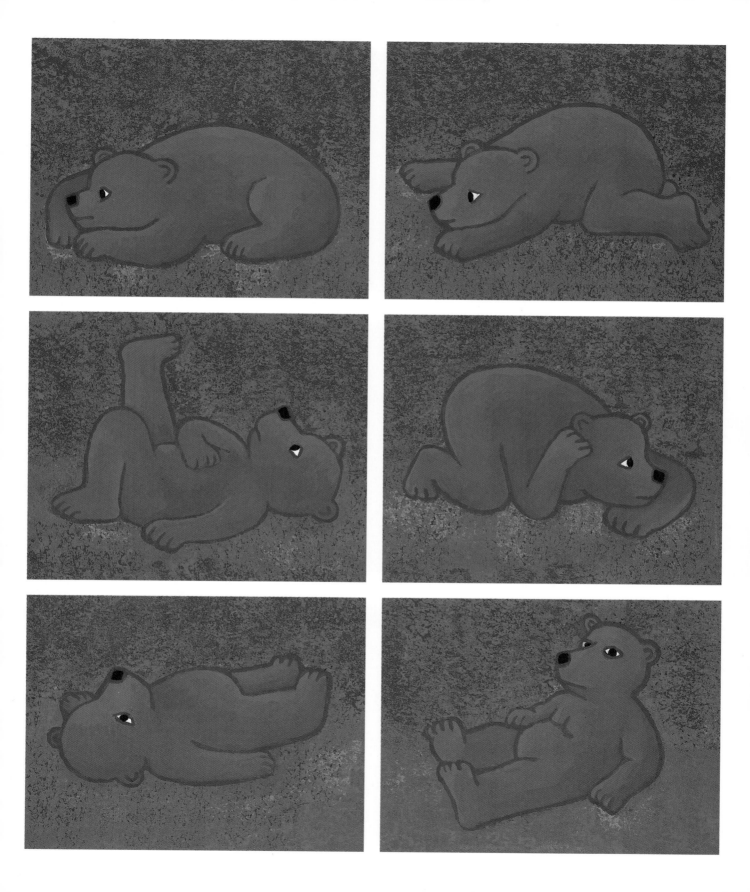

He poked Mother Bear and said, "Mama, I'm thirsty."
"I'm sorry," replied Mother Bear. "There's no water
in the cave."

"But I always had a drink before I went to sleep when we slept under the stars," said Baby Bear.

"Okay," sighed Mother Bear. "Stay here, and I'll see what I can do."

Mother Bear followed the scent of water until it led her to a small stream. She dipped some leaves into the water and carried them back to Baby Bear.

"Thank you, Mama," said Baby Bear as he licked the water from the leaves. "Maybe *now* I'll sleep."

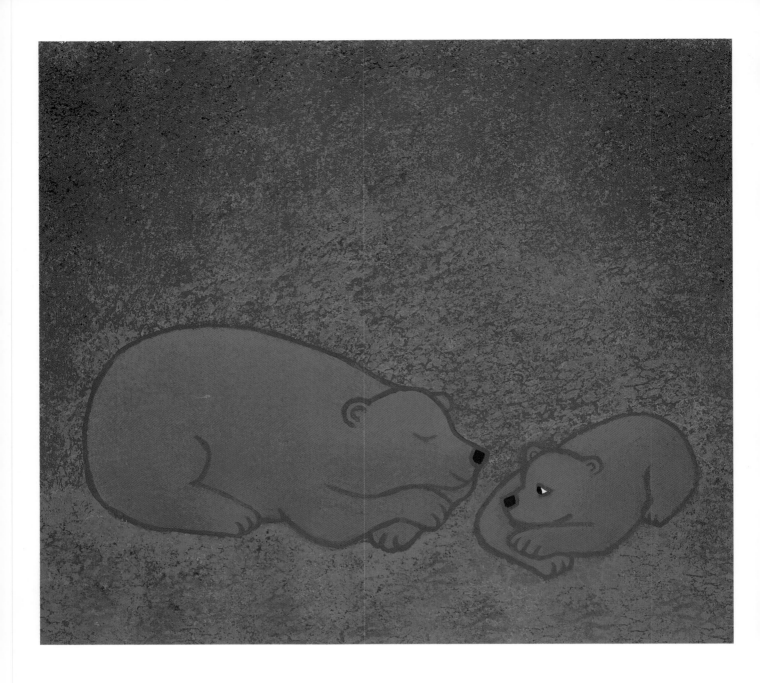

Baby Bear lay down next to Mother Bear and waited
to fall asleep.
He waited and waited and thought and thought.

Then he bumped Mother Bear and said, "Mama, you know what I need? I need the moon."

"You need *what*?" gasped Mother Bear.

"I never have trouble falling asleep when I can look at the moon," explained Baby Bear.

"I can't get you the moon," cried Mother Bear.

"But I *need* it!" insisted Baby Bear.

Mother Bear heaved a great sigh. "Wait here," she said, and lumbered out of the cave.

By now the snow had stopped falling and the moon was out. Its light fell on the snow like warm honey.

"Oh, Moon!" Mother Bear called to the sky. "I'm so tired and my baby can't fall asleep without you. What am I to do?"

Just then some snow from a pine tree fell onto the
hillside and began to roll. As it rolled it gathered more
snow and grew bigger and bigger. By the time it reached
Mother Bear, it looked as big and round as the moon.

"Thank you, Moon," said Mother Bear. And she rolled the snowball into the cave.

"I know it's not the moon," she said. "But there's just enough moonlight coming into the cave to make it shine like the moon. Can you see it?"

"Oh yes!" cried Baby Bear.
"Good," said Mother Bear. "Now *please* go to sleep."

"Okay, Mama," said Baby Bear. "Just one more thing."
"What now?" grumbled Mother Bear.

"I want to give you a kiss," said Baby Bear, and he kissed Mother Bear on the nose.

"Good night, Baby Bear," murmured Mother Bear. She drew her cub into a warm embrace and kissed him back.

"Good night, Mama," said Baby Bear, and he closed his eyes. And this time, deep beneath the snow in his cozy, warm cave, Baby Bear fell asleep.